THIS 📖 BELONGS TO

Mostly Mary

Mostly Mary

A Mary Plain Adventure

GWYNEDD RAE
CLARA VULLIAMY

EGMONT

EGMONT

We bring stories to life

First published in Great Britain 1930.
This edition first published in Great Britain 2017 by Egmont UK Limited
The Yellow Building, 1 Nicholas Road, London W11 4AN
www.egmont.co.uk

ISBN 978 1 4052 8122 5

A CIP catalogue record for this title is available from the British Library.

MIX
Paper
FSC FSC® C018306

THIS  IS FOR

THE 🦉 MAN BECOS

HE WAS SO KIND

🖐 FOR LEAH BECOS

SHE FOUND ME W🐔

I WAS A LOST 🐖

Contents

Foreword

by Clara Vulliamy, 2017

I have loved Mary Plain since I was very young, and have longed to illustrate her stories ever since I could first properly hold a pencil.

The books were read to me by my mother, the author and illustrator Shirley Hughes, whose own mother read them to her, and I in turn have read them to my children. Iconic Mary-isms have entered our family language. We plan 'svisits' instead of visits, and write notes to each other in Mary picture writing. When uncertain, sad or homesick, we find Mary's wobbly words, 'Do you think the twins are happy without me?', say it better than anything else could.

Gwynedd Rae's creation is an orphan bear cub from the bear pits of Berne Zoo. Mary is both bear-like and child-like, a perfect combination, an enormous personality all wrapped up in a small, pointy-eared, browny-grey furry package. Mary can be wilful, cheeky and impossible, with an unsquashable ego and an insatiable appetite. But she is also funny, irrepressibly optimistic and utterly endearing.

I love the world of the bear pits and Mary's extended family that inhabit it – the grumpy older bears and her twin cousins Little Wool and Marionetta. They fall out and make up, just like all families.

Written between 1930 and 1965, the Mary Plain series has an abundance of delightful vintage details throughout. But the universal appeal of the escapades and hijinks of a small bear cub, at large in the sophisticated world of grown-ups, is timeless.

There has been a Mary-shaped gap in the cast list of classic bears in children's books for far too long. I'm so proud and happy to see the enchanting and entertaining writings of Gwynedd Rae restored, and for Mary to become a wonderful companion for another generation of readers. She doesn't need any help to introduce herself, so, in her own words . . .

'I am Mary Plain, an unusual first-class bear
with a white rosette and a gold medal
with a picture of myself on it.'

The Introduction

by Gwynedd Rae, 1930

The following is a story about my friends, the Berne bears, who are *real* bears, and not just Teddies.

A few years ago I was obliged to spend most of the winter months at Berne and I began to look around for some interest. I found it at once in these bears, who live in a pit there, and who were, from the very first, an immense joy and amusement to me.

I must explain in a few words their history.

An old legend runs that, as far back as 1191, a certain duke built himself a fortress to protect himself from his enemies, and this same fortress gradually grew into a small fortified town.

One day, hunting near by, he killed a bear, and named the town after it – Berne – now the capital of Switzerland, which still has a bear as its coat of arms.

It was as long ago as 1513 that the Bernese first kept some bears in a pit, and ever since, all through the centuries, they have done the same.

They are extremely proud of these animals, and at

all times and in all weathers you will see an affectionate audience leaning over the wall, feeding them with carrots, biscuits or figs.

There were nine bears when I was there, and they were divided into three pits, which I have called The Den, Parlour Pit and the Nursery. I have also drawn a little plan to make it easier to understand about their home.

I would add that, though I have written this small book, I know nothing whatsoever about the bears' real lives and habits; only, through my many visits to them, they have become my friends, each with their own separate character. So I have written down some things about them, and I feel sure that some of the many children who love bears, will agree with me that they might easily be true.

The Bear Family Tree

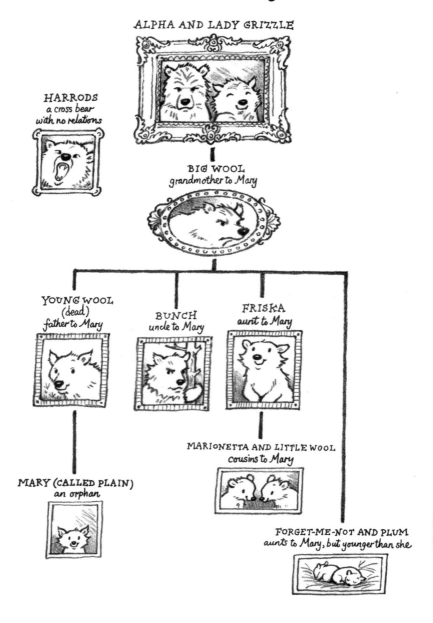

ALPHA AND LADY GRIZZLE

HARRODS
*a cross bear
with no relations*

BIG WOOL
grandmother to Mary

YOUNG WOOL
(dead)
father to Mary

BUNCH
uncle to Mary

FRISKA
aunt to Mary

MARIONETTA AND LITTLE WOOL
cousins to Mary

MARY (CALLED PLAIN)
an orphan

FORGET-ME-NOT AND PLUM
aunts to Mary, but younger than she

. . . and Friends

THE OWL MAN

THE FANCY-COAT-LADY

JOB AND MRS JOB

THE GREY LADY

The Home of the Bears
The Bear Pits, Berne Zoo

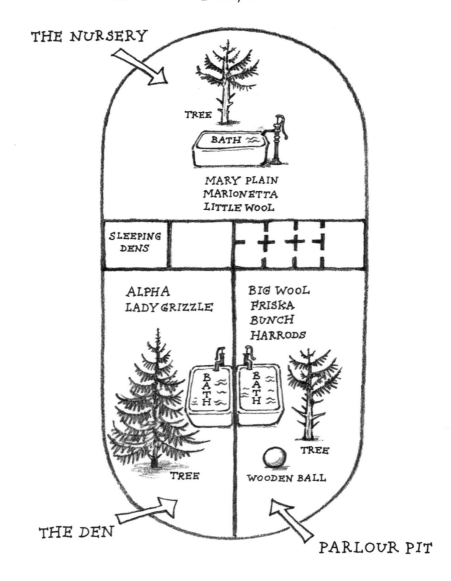

THE NURSERY

TREE

BATH

MARY PLAIN
MARIONETTA
LITTLE WOOL

SLEEPING
DENS

ALPHA
LADY GRIZZLE

BIG WOOL
FRISKA
BUNCH
HARRODS

BATH

BATH

TREE

TREE

WOODEN BALL

THE DEN

PARLOUR PIT

Chapter One

In which we get to know the bears

Mary was six months old. She had rather pointed ears, and she lived in Nursery Pit, with her twin cousins, Marionetta and Little Wool. The twins had nice black coats, but Mary's was a kind of browny-grey, but she did not mind much, as she said to herself sensibly, 'At least we can't get mixed up.'

Mary was not sensible about many things, but this was one of the few exceptions. Being an orphan, she had had to bring herself up, more or less, and she had on the whole done a good job of it. She was usually in some kind of trouble, but she was quite used to that, and supposed that orphan bears were born different from the rest, so that was why she was always just a little less lucky than the others.

The twins' mother, Friska, lived next door in Parlour Pit with her mother, Big Wool, her brother, Bunch, and Harrods, a cross old bear who was called this because she looked like the kind of bear you might see in a toy shop.

Friska was a nice sensible bear, very good-tempered and a great help to her mother. She was very different from her brother. Bunch was lazy and greedy and thought he was much the most important bear in the world.

Big Wool had done her best to get rid of these bad habits when Bunch was a cub, but she gave it up in the end, because it was a waste of breath and did no good at all. As far as looks went she could not help being rather proud of him, as he had a lovely dark coat which stood out in a thick ruff round his neck – but his manners were a great sorrow to her.

In Parlour Pit there was a big fir-tree in the middle, with branches all broken off to stumps where the bears had climbed, and on the side of the pit was a big square bath full of running water, where they drank and had their baths on Wednesday afternoons.

There were also big iron doors which were pulled by chains, leading to the sleeping dens, but these were always kept shut during the day, as it was a very strict rule that no bear was allowed to go to his den for a midday rest, however tired he might be. He just *had* to make the best of the pit floor.

In Den Pit, which was the last of the three, lived Alpha and Lady Grizzle. They were so old that they could not climb their tree, which was the only one that still had beautiful shady green branches – just what they needed to rest under when the sun was too warm to be really comfortable. They were so ancient and wise that all the other bears were in awe of them and they were kept separate from the rest, having their own dens to sleep in; and only once a year, on St Bruin's Day, which is the great bear festival, the younger ones all went to visit them and took them a small present.

One sunny morning in early autumn, Friska was busy getting all the bowls clean and ready for breakfast, which would be brought at any moment. She licked them all with great care, and then gave them a final polish round with her paw. She sighed when she came to Bunch's bowl, it was always so clean – no stray bits of meat or bran to provide a rather empty bear with a little courage till breakfast time arrived.

Just as Friska finished the last bowl she heard Job undoing the chain on the door. For a long time the bears had not known his name, and they had always called him 'the kind breakfast and supper man' – rather a long name for one person. One morning he was having a lot of trouble raking up the straw to make their beds, which were in a great mess. Mary

happened to be in the corner
conscious and hoping no awkw
be asked – for the truth was tha
had had a splendid pillow-fight

However, he only grumbled a l
place, and said, 'You're more tr
pack of children, and it's a lucky thing my name's
Job,' and Mary heard and ran off to tell Friska what
his real name was.

Breakfast was, somehow, a very hungry meal –
at least the bears thought so. Through the day they
had plenty to eat, because so many grown-ups and
children came to visit them, and threw them carrots
and biscuits, or any other odds and ends they had
collected and brought in a paper bag. But they found
it a long time to wait from supper-time till breakfast –
especially Bunch, who got restless towards daylight
and began to twist about and mutter in
his sleep, which was rather
disturbing to the older bears,
who were not quite as tight
asleep as the babies.

...y after breakfast, Big Wool clapped her ...and said, 'Now then, all of you in a row – ...ick!' And all the bears hurried to their places in order of size – first Harrods, then Friska, Bunch, Little Wool, Marionetta and finally Mary, the babiest of them all.

'Faces!' said Big Wool, and every bear licked its paws and smoothed the fur on its face.

'Ears!' and then all the paws moved busily from mouth to ear, smoothing and patting. All but Mary's, who found the whole cleaning and tidying business boring and thought that ears, especially, should be left in peace.

'Mary!' said Big Wool sternly. Mary gave a quick lick and pat and fiddled half-heartedly with an ear – just till Big Wool looked away again.

'Chests!' and this was the part that Mary quite enjoyed – because it meant straining back one's neck to reach, and Mary would see how far back she could lean without going over, and it nearly always ended in her going just a little further than she could.

As soon as this was over, Bunch would hurry to the door, so as to be the first to reach the tree. He was very selfish about the tree and did not like any other bear to come on to it. Not that any of them wanted to, but Bunch pretended to himself that they did, for it made a far better game. Sometimes he would come down to the bottom of the tree and stand with his two front paws still on the lowest branch, looking very ready for a quarrel, and, if any of the others came within a metre of him he would rush up the tree again, making a lovely Bunch noise through his nose. It was a kind of loud, snuffly roar and he kept it specially for this occasion.

He was an intelligent bear, because he had chosen that branch, just in front of and level with the carrot stall because he knew that anyone buying carrots and turning round, would find him in a beautiful position exactly opposite, clapping his stiff paws for the first one.

He also knew very well that only the heavy

carrots reached him there, the small ones fell short, so, though some people were bad throwers and he missed a good many, when one did reach him, it was sure to be a nice, big, juicy one, well worth the catching and the eating. Big Wool had warned him many times that he would lose his figure if he ate so much, but he just shrugged his shoulders and ate all the more. Bunch was like that.

Chapter Two

All about school and rather short

School was held very early, before the iron doors were closed and the bears separated for the day.

Friska rattled the chain on the door which was the signal for the cubs to come running to their places. They sat in a row along the edge of the bath, which made an excellent bench, and Friska stood in front of them.

Only the three little ones had lessons, and Mary thought with longing of the time when she would be so big and clever that she would have nothing more to learn.

One day the twins were having rather an argument about who had been at the top of the class when lessons had ended the day before. This never worried Mary, for she had never even been in the middle, so she was standing under the wall and chatting to a robin who had been pecking near the railings up above.

Friska looked up and saw the sun was getting very near the tree tops which meant it was late, so she gave a sudden deep growl. 'To your seats, please.' At the same moment she leant forward and gave Mary a prod which made her jump and then scramble off to her seat as quick as quick.

By this time the twins had changed places so often that they had worked their way to the end of the seat, and, when Mary, still looking over her shoulder at Friska, reached her place next to the twins, she sat down – just beyond where the seat ended! The cement was very hard and Mary had quite a temper, and before anyone had time to do anything she was up again and flying at the cubs in a fury, and she pushed them deliberately backwards into the bath.

They gasped and gulped and climbed out like drowned rats, looking the picture of misery, because the sun had not had time to warm the water, and it was not Wednesday, their bath day, anyway.

Now, Friska was a wise bear and, though she knew it had all been a mistake, she felt she could not let it pass. So she ordered her two cubs to run up and down in the sun to dry themselves, at the same time telling them that because they had argued so much, they would have no sugar after supper.

Then she called Mary to her and said, 'I expect you are sorry, already, that you have been so unkind to your little cousins, but –'

'No – I'm not at all,' said Mary rudely, because she was still very sore.

'But,' went on Friska firmly, 'you will be far more sorry when I explain to you that it was all a mistake. They had no idea that, while quarrelling, they had moved so far up the seat and had left no room for you. Also –'

'I –' began Mary.

'Also, also, also,' said Friska very quickly so that Mary could not interrupt, 'even if they had done it on purpose, it wasn't at all right to push them into the water – especially after the bad cold Little Wool had last week. So, although I know you only did it because you were hurt and angry, I am going to send you into the corner for ten minutes, so you will have time to think over how sorry you will be if, through your fault, Little Wool gets pneumonia.'

Mary went off happily. She had no idea what pneumonia was, but she did not in the least mind if Little Wool got two of it. Nor did she feel ashamed when she heard him sneeze, but lay down on her back and started the game she had invented with her four paws, which passed the time splendidly.

'Come along, you two!' called Friska. 'You must

be nearly dry now. Sit down quietly and concentrate on your lessons, or you'll find yourselves in the other two corners – besides having no sugar.'

'Yes, mamma,' they said and sat down with their paws folded demurely.

Friska began the first lesson.

'A for –?'

'Alpha!' said Little Wool.

'Good! C for –?'

'Carrots,' said Little Wool again.

'Right! Come along, Marionetta. Don't let your little brother do all the answering. F for –?'

'Figska!' said Mary unexpectedly from her corner. The paw game had begun to get a bit dull and she was sitting up and listening.

Friska took no notice. 'F for –?'

'Food!' said Marionetta at last.

'P for –?'

Marionetta looked at Mary and then said 'Punishment!' very loud.

'Pig!' flashed Mary and stuck out her tongue. But when Friska turned round to see if she had heard right, Mary had her back to her and seemed very interested in a crack in the wall – so she thought she must have been mistaken.

'S for –?'

'Sugar,' moaned the twins. Mary turned round quickly.

'S for stout,' she said deliberately, and then felt frightened for she knew that Friska was very anxious *not* to grow stout. Friska looked at her and Mary held her breath. Then after a long moment she turned back and continued.

'G for –?'

'Good,' said Mary quickly, much relieved.

Now all these interruptions were not helping the class, so Friska decided they should end.

'If Mary is now going to be good,' she said, 'she may come and join in the lessons.'

Mary came, running, and sat down.

'W for –?'

'Wuffle,' said Mary. The other two giggled.

'What', said Friska coldly, 'is a wuffle?'

'I thought perhaps you could tell me,' said Mary innocently.

Friska decided to let this pass, as she felt perhaps she ought to know what a wuffle was.

'M for –?'

'Me!' said Mary brightly. 'Me *and* Mary, Mary *and* me – both of us.'

There was no denying the truth of this, so Friska cleared her throat and said, 'We will now have some arithmetic. How many carrots make a bunch?'

'Eight,' said Marionetta.

'Nine,' said Little Wool.

'It all depends,' said Mary and she was right.

'Ten in season and six out of season,' explained Friska, 'and don't forget. How many bears are there in this pit?'

'Four,' said the twins.

'Three,' said Mary.

'How many did you say, Mary?'

'Three, Auntie,' she said modestly. 'I felt perhaps I ought not to count myself as I'd been naughty.'

And at that moment, to Friska's great relief, Job called down that she must hurry into Parlour Pit, as he was going to let the doors down – so that ended lessons for that day.

Chapter Three

Of how Mary found her missing name

Mary was sitting on the side of the bath hugging herself. She was so happy that she would gladly have hugged somebody else, but as there were only the twins handy and she knew they would hate it, she had to do the best she could with herself. Being an orphan, and the others being twins, Mary sometimes could not help feeling a little lonely; for though they were all very friendly on the whole, the others naturally played together and not always games for three. So she had lots of time to think, and she had spent quite a lot of it thinking about her name.

Her name was a great sorrow to her. She felt that it was so very short, and this had made her, each time she thought about it, rather sad – though she had far too much pride to show it.

Little Wool had two names and Marionetta, though she had only one, had at least a good long one; but Mary – just Mary – seemed such a very small name to have. She had often wondered whether, as she was the youngest bear, there perhaps had not been enough names to go round; but she had never quite liked to ask.

And on this afternoon a most wonderful thing had happened, and she could never remember being so glad about anything before.

She had a special friend, a kind lady, who wore a fancy coat and gave her carrots and really seemed to take an interest in her jumping efforts, because she was the only cub that could jump and she was very proud of it. Well, she had been standing looking wistfully up at the lady, with Little Wool and Marionetta beside her, when she saw her friend lean over the railings, and, as she dropped a nice orange carrot, say '*Isn't* Mary plain?'

Mary was so startled that she let the carrot lie

unnoticed at her feet, and Little Wool pulled it to him with his paw and gobbled it up. But Marionetta had heard and said in an excited voice, 'Mary, did you hear? That lady called you "Mary Plain". Is it your name?'

Mary pulled herself together. 'Yes,' she said, 'didn't you know?' Then she walked away casually, and hoped they wouldn't notice how her heart was thumping in her side.

As soon as the twins had moved away a little, she hurried back to her friend and did three of her very best jumps running to show how grateful she was. She felt somehow taller, and less lonely already, and the more she thought of it, the more excited she got inside, till at last she felt she must do something to work it off, or she would burst. So she suddenly ran up and gave Marionetta a soft box on the ear and cried, 'Can't catch me!' and then of course Marionetta had to show she could, and there followed a tremendous game of "Catch" round and round the pit – dodging round the bath and behind the tree into the corner, till at last Mary was caught, because Little Wool had joined Marionetta explaining that it was completely fair and not two against one, as they were twins. Mary, panting hard, had no breath and no real wish to contradict them, so she waited a moment, and then said she'd be 'It'.

Off they went again, tearing after each other, while all the people looking over the wall laughed and clapped.

It ended in a very flat way for Mary – and not for the first time. Just as she was going to catch her, Marionetta gave a big spring and scrambled up the tree, leaving poor Mary down below, looking longingly up at her, because Mary could not climb the tree. Nor could Little Wool for that matter, which was a comfort, but Marionetta could, and showed off abominably over it.

Nothing, however, could really make Mary feel unhappy that day – she felt too bubbly inside – so she and Little Wool had a rolling match and Mary won, and it was great fun, and before they knew where they were it was time to go to bed.

Except in the case of the two very old bears, all the sleeping dens connected inside, and though there was one for each bear, the three cubs nearly always crept into one and snuggled up together. They took it in turns to be in the middle and on cold nights they rolled

up so tightly that they looked like balls of wool.

On this night Mary could not settle for a long time. She kept being so happy about having two names, that it made her very wide awake. She turned this way and that, and through her head ran the happenings of this most thrilling day. She started at the beginning and went over them all again, and when she got to where Marionetta had sprung up the tree she began to puzzle, as she often had before, how she did it.

It was such a smooth tree till far further up than she could reach – only some flattish bumps that you could not catch hold of. So, till she could be tall enough to reach the first branch, how could she ever hope to get up the tree? Then, quite suddenly, she had a brilliant idea.

She thought: 'When I want a carrot, I jump for it, and if I jump enough times, I get it. So if I want very badly, as I do, to get up that tree, I shall get up if I jump enough, because jumping always gives me what I want.' Which, though it sounds a little muddling, was quite plain to Mary. So she decided she really must put it to the test, and while she was wondering why she had never thought of it before, she fell sound asleep.

Luckily Little Wool had a nightmare towards morning and he gave Mary such a violent kick that it woke her. She was just going to be very angry about it, when she remembered that to be woken early was just exactly what she wanted; so she got up and crept carefully out into the nursery.

It was still almost dark and she felt very grown-up at being up all alone – and oh! she wanted so badly to be able to say to Marionetta, 'I can climb that tree too – so there!'

She crept up to it and then, with a heart full of hope, she stood up beside it and started jumping. She jumped till her breath came in short pants and her front paws felt too heavy to lift. Then she took a little rest and started again – always with eyes uplifted, waiting for the blissful moment when she would find herself on that branch. How comfortable it looked! The thought gave her fresh strength. She made no effort to touch the tree – just jumped. But, alas, after a little time more, she ached all over and her hind legs were shaking and she felt bitterly disappointed.

At last she had to acknowledge it was just not any good. Here she still was at the bottom of the tree, very tired, very hungry, and no better off than before. She was, indeed, tired out, and without knowing it she fell asleep there and then, and Big Wool found her a few hours later.

'Whatever is this cub doing here?' she said and woke her.

Mary sat up and rubbed her eyes and Big Wool said,

'My dear child, how did you get here?'

'I – I c-can't think,' stammered Mary, very embarrassed, because it had all flashed back to her.

'Perhaps you walked in your sleep?' suggested Big Wool.

'Yes – perhaps I did,' said Mary gratefully, and so it was settled.

Chapter Four

Which belongs chiefly to Bunch

Mary Plain was not the only bear who had a special friend, but Bunch's was a man, known as the 'Owl Man' because of the dark circles he wore round his eyes.

He and Bunch had many long talks together; in fact he was the only person that Bunch talked to much at all.

To be honest the Owl Man was unfair about the carrots, because he gave the most to Bunch. This after all, as he was Bunch's special friend, was forgivable, but the other bears felt that he might at least have pretended to be a little interested in them from time to time, just for politeness's sake, especially as practice had made him a very good shot. Very few carrots fell below; and anyway, the others did not have quite the same sense of enjoyment in eating Bunch's 'misses', as the carrots they had themselves caught with some skill.

The Owl Man had not been to pay a visit for two days, so Bunch was very pleased to see him come round the corner, one afternoon. To his surprise, instead of walking straight up to the carrot stall as usual, he turned aside just before and leant over the wall.

'Good morning, Bunch!' he said.

'Good afternoon,' said Bunch.

'There's something I want to ask you.'

'Oh?' said Bunch.

'And I'm hoping you will approve.'

'Oh?' said Bunch again.

'It's a little difficult to explain.'

'Oh?' said Bunch and yawned – which was neither encouraging nor polite – so the Owl Man took the bull by the horns and said, 'Do you like milk?'

'No,' said Bunch. This was a very large lie, but he was tired of listening to all these rather dull remarks and wished the Owl Man would get on with the buying of his carrots.

This answer was obviously a blow, and the Owl Man looked very disappointed.

'You're quite sure about it? Not even condensed?'

'No!'

'*And* sweetened?'

'No!' Bunch was determined to be difficult, so the Owl Man got just a little annoyed.

'Well – I'm sorry,' he said bluntly, 'because I was hoping you'd get down off that tree and come and stand underneath me here, and let me pour some NICE – SWEET – SUGARY – *STICKY* milk down your throat,' (here Bunch licked his lips). 'But I realize that nothing will budge you from that tree of yours, so I shall just give it to the other bears, who – who have more sense,' he finished with anger.

Bunch suddenly had a wish to break his rule and get down – just for once – but no, it would not do; once might lead to many times. So he forced himself to say, coldly, 'I prefer carrots.'

'Oh – but –' said the Owl Man, 'I'm sorry to say I've come without my wallet, so I can't buy you any carrots and it's milk or nothing! And I am going to start now!'

As he said this Bunch's legs started to come down of their own accord, but he stopped them quickly and pretended he'd just wanted to change his position a bit.

This was serious. He had not at all understood that the milk was to be *instead* of the carrots, and it had never occurred to him that he would not get his bunch as usual. How very careless of the Owl Man to forget his wallet! And he looked away quickly as he saw a long white stream pouring into Friska's eager mouth. He felt that it would have been kinder of his late friend, at least, to have chosen a spot a little further away and not directly opposite him. He tried hard to keep his attention fixed on a distant tree, but 'sugary', 'sweet', 'sticky' and other equally attractive words would float disturbingly into his mind, and his lips seemed curiously dry that afternoon.

It was nearly over the next time he looked, and what a mess they were all in – covered with white sticky stuff – a really disgusting sight. And it was so bad for the coat, he felt sure; in fact he got so worried about the harm it might do his mother's coat, who seemed in the worst state, that he seriously thought of getting down and offering to clean it for her. After all he was her only son, and perhaps he had not been thoughtful enough of her lately. He was wavering like this, when he saw the Owl Man preparing to go, so he decided to stay where he was, for now at any rate, till he was out of the way.

The Owl Man was wiping his hands on his handkerchief and Bunch hoped that the stickiness would not come off. He finished at last and to Bunch's surprise, instead of going, he leaned over the wall and smiled at him.

'Well, did you really think I was going away without giving you anything? But I couldn't resist teasing you! It's quite true, I have left my wallet behind and I can't buy you any carrots, but how would some sugar do instead? I happen to have a lump or two in my pocket.'

Now Bunch had meant to be very offhand and not at all ready to make friends again, after the thoughtless way he had been treated that afternoon, but at the sound of that magic word 'sugar' he could not, for the life of him, control his ears – they just *would* stand up.

'Come along!' went on the Owl Man. 'Cheer up! Let's shake hands on it and be friends again and here goes the first lump – as a sign of peace!' And he threw a square white lump right into Bunch's mouth, which happened to be open, and by the time the fifth lump had disappeared Bunch had forgotten his resentment and they were friends once more.

When his friend had gone, Bunch turned his attention back to his mother. Though Big Wool had been licking away as hard as she could and Friska had very kindly helped her, she was still in a great mess. Just as Bunch was wondering how she would ever get clean again, Big Wool settled the matter herself by deciding to take a bath, so Bunch's mind was relieved, and he arranged himself comfortably on his branch and soon forgot all about her.

Big Wool was really glad of the excuse for a bath, for she enjoyed bathing hugely. She was so big that, when she got right into the bath, the water overflowed all over the sides, and she splashed such enormous splashes that everything nearby was drenched. She washed all four paws very thoroughly while she floated on her back, and then she rinsed her head under the running spout of water.

Friska was not afraid of enjoying a game when her cubs were not there to see her, and she became quite jolly and full of fun. She would go up to Big Wool and nibble her neck and tease her, till Big Wool would pretend to be angry and plunge out of the bath after her and they would lumber round and round the pit like two big babies. There was a big wooden ball in the pit, and Big Wool had great games with this, tossing it about in the water, hiding it with one paw, and then finding it with the other. Sometimes she would throw it out of the bath and then heave herself out after it and fetch it back. Once it rolled right into the corner where Harrods was lying and trying, as usual, to go to sleep.

Now Harrods was a disagreeable old bear; no one really liked her because she was jealous and cross, and always spoilt the fun. Bunch and Friska were continually getting into trouble with her, and Big Wool was the only one who could manage her at all. When the ball rolled past her and Big Wool came after it, Harrods sprang up snarling, and looked as if she would attack her if she went any further.

Big Wool pulled up short when she saw her face. 'I've lost my ball, Harrods,' she said politely.

'Grrrrr,' growled Harrods.

'I think I saw it roll this way,' went on Big Wool.

'Grrr –, Grrr –,' growled Harrods.

'Oh yes – there it is – I'll just get it.' But Harrods barred her way, with teeth bared, and paw uplifted.

Big Wool stood still and then she said, quite quietly, 'Do you like cake?' and, as she spoke, Harrods put her paw down and moved on one side, and Big Wool went forward and got her ball, with no further fuss.

Now the explanation of the curious hold Big Wool had over Harrods is this –

A long time before, when Friska was just a cub, she was having a birthday (bears always have two birthdays every year) and she was very excited because her mamma had told her she was going to have a party that evening, and there would be a lovely surprise.

Friska was a particular favourite with Mrs Job, who kept the carrot stall, so when she heard she was having a birthday, she had very kindly made her a lovely cake, with pink icing and three candles – fixed in a little wooden stand, sitting on top – and sent it to the bear, by her husband, that morning.

Big Wool was delighted and hid it carefully under the straw in her den till the evening, so it would be safe. Job had promised that, as soon as the den doors were opened after sun-down, he would put it in the middle of the floor in Big Wool's den, which was the biggest, and light the candles.

Just as they were all getting ready, Friska, who was having a wrestling match with Bunch, fell over and bumped her head very hard against the wall. She was a little over-excited, which was natural, so wasn't quite as brave as usual, and Big Wool had to come and rub her head for her.

As soon as she stopped crying, her mother hurried off to see if all was ready. She went into her den and could hardly believe her eyes. The cake had gone – entirely disappeared! Only the candles were left burning in their stand and behind them stood Harrods, licking her lips. Big Wool could have cried, only she was far too angry – so angry that she did not dare trust herself to speak – so she just gave one terrible growl at the thief, who shrank back into the corner, ashamed. Then she had to think quickly how to make the party fun without a cake, so that poor Friska's birthday would not be completely spoilt.

She had no other food. The only thing to do was to make the most of the candles, so she went to the door and said in an excited voice, 'You can come in now, Friska, and look at the lovely stars we have caught for your birthday.'

Friska came bounding in, walked round the table and then stopped and sniffed. Perhaps she couldn't help being just a tiny bit disappointed that there seemed to be nothing to eat.

But just then Big Wool cried, 'Oh what a lucky girl to have such a lovely party! Three bright stars, all especially for Friska – *such* a treat! None of us ever had stars for our birthdays before!' And she made them all join hands, all except Harrods, who had slunk away to hide her shame in her own den, and they hopped round and round the tree singing, 'Oh, lucky Friska! Oh, lucky Friska!' till Friska began to think it *was* rather a nice thing to have stars for presents after all; and when, at the end, Big Wool led her up and showed her how to blow them out, she was sure of it.

Big Wool must have had a very firm talk with Harrods that night, and threatened to tell everybody, because ever since that day, whenever Harrods is being tiresome, Big Wool has only to say, in a certain tone of voice, 'Do you like cake?' and Harrods behaves at once.

Chapter Five

Which is white with snow

The days were getting shorter and shorter and sometimes it was very cold. One morning Mary ran to the door and gave a cry.

'Oh, Twins, come and look! The ground is all covered with white; do you think a cloud has tumbled down?'

The twins rushed out to see, and when they too had said 'Oh!' a great many times, they looked up and saw that the trees were white too, so decided it could not be a cloud.

'Could it possibly be sugar?' said Mary hopefully.

'Shall I try?' and she bent down and licked the strange white stuff. 'No,' she said disappointedly, 'it's not, and it doesn't taste of anything but wet.'

Their cries had brought Big Wool and Friska to the door and they had been standing behind them and listening with amusement to their conversation.

Big Wool said, 'That's snow, cubs! Didn't you know?'

'The twins didn't,' said Mary, a little unfairly.

Then the older ones showed them how to roll the snow up into balls and they had the best morning of their lives, playing splendid games, because the snow was about ten centimetres deep, and they didn't feel the cold in their nice fur coats.

Marionetta chased Little Wool with such a big snowball that he fled out of her way, and, in his hurry, tripped and fell backwards over the edge of the bath, but imagine his surprise, when, instead of the wetting he expected, he found himself lying *on* the water, in the middle of the tank. Was he dreaming, or floating, or what had happened? He called to Marionetta cautiously, 'Do you mind just feeling the water at the edge of the bath?'

Marionetta did. 'I can't put my paw in it,' she said. 'It's completely hard!'

'Are you sure it's hard there, too?'

'Yes! How funny! Are you *on* the water, Little Wool?'

'Yes, I am. And I'm going to get off!' But this wasn't quite as easy as he thought, because every time he got carefully to his feet, they somehow left him. Try as he would, he could not stop them, and there he was, flat on his back again. He got rather hot and bothered, especially as Mary had joined Marionetta, and they were both standing beside the bath, shouting with laughter.

'It doesn't *feel* funny,' said Little Wool, as he landed on the ice with a bang for the tenth time. 'Can't you two suggest something, instead of standing there laughing?'

'I can't help it,' gasped Mary. 'Do you really want to get off? Because if you'd just go on trying to get up a few more times, it's such – such fun!' she finished hysterically.

But Marionetta was a twin, and so, though she couldn't quite stop laughing however hard she thought of dead beetles and empty breakfast bowls, she leant over as far as she could reach and said, 'If you stretch out your paw as far as you can, I think I could pull you out.'

And she did. Little Wool didn't feel very dignified being pulled along on his back, but he didn't really mind too much what happened, as long as he got on solid ground again.

Later on they made a huge snowball bigger than themselves, and Mary cried, 'Oh, it's like a man.'

'But without eyes and nose,' said the twins.

'I know,' shouted Mary, and she went and stood under a kind-looking old lady and jumped, and for each jump she gave Mary a dried fig. When Mary had collected three, she picked them all up and ran back, fixed them in the snowman's face for two eyes, and a mouth; and then the twins rushed off and got a carrot, which was perfect for a nose.

After a while Mary got tired of playing with the snowman, who was beginning to melt, because the sun was very warm, and she noticed a stone lying near the bath, which was long and pointed. She picked it up and sat down on the side of the bath and began dragging it up and down on the ice. To her surprise it made a lovely mark, so she started to write, and as she did not know how to spell many words, she drew pictures of them instead, and this is what she wrote:

[eye] AM A SMALL [pig] & I LIVE IN A PIT
& U CANT C MUCH OUTSIDE XCEPT [bushes] &
LOTS OF [people] WHO R VERY KIND & BRING US
[carrots] 2 EAT & 1/3 TIMES 4 A [cow]E TREAT
2/3 [dice] . I HAVE A [bath] ALWAYS ON
WENDSDAY & SOME[clock]S ON OTHER DAYS
W[hen] THE [sun] IS SHINING & WE

SIT AND GET DRY.
I HAVE A OF AND HAVE A
OF MY OWN 2 HAVE MY BREAKFAST &
ONCE WE MADE A & HE WAS VERY
ROUND AND HE TURNED 2 & I WAS SAD
& THIS IS ALL T I HAVE TO
SAY XCEPT THAT MY NAME IS

MARY

Mary sat back and looked at it, and was pleased. She strolled over to the twins and said, 'I've written a book on the bath, about me. I don't mind you reading it, if you want to very badly, just for once.'

The twins rushed over to look. 'But it's half pictures!' they cried. 'How clever of you to make pictures!'

'Oh, it's quite easy,' said Mary, trying to look modest. 'Would you like me to write a book about you?'

'Oh please! Oh yes!' they shouted. So Mary wrote:

LITTLE WOOL'S 👁 👁 R D🛥 AND HIS 🐕 IS P🍳.

Little Wool jumped up and down with excitement and cried, 'What have you said about me, Mary Plain?' Mary told him, and he said, 'Oh, is it?' and stuck out his tongue to see.

'Now me, now me,' cried Marionetta, so Mary wrote:

MARIONETTA 12 $\frac{1}{3}$ $\frac{}{4}$ TIMES 🍲 PID AT HER ABC DEF GHI

and when she told her what she had written Marionetta was not at all pleased and said, 'I'm not.'

'I said "sometimes",' said Mary.

'But I'm not *ever*, I'm very clever, and I shall write it underneath.'

'Do,' said Mary, and handed her the stone.

Marionetta took it and held it ready to write just off the ice, but, after she had wriggled it to and fro a few times she threw it down and said, 'No, I don't feel like it now.'

'Just as you like,' said Mary, and was secretly very pleased, because she knew perfectly well that Marionetta did not know how to write.

She waited till she moved away and then wrote:

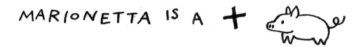

but it did not matter, because when the twins looked at it later on, they decided it was a picture of Bunch.

The next two days were not as much fun, because the sun had shone so hard that the lovely white snow had turned to muddy water. Although the cubs enjoyed paddling, poor Mary woke up next morning with a swollen face and bad toothache. She spent a very miserable day, curled up in a ball in a patch of sun, which had dried a corner of the pit, and she didn't want to play, or catch carrots, or anything.

That evening, as soon as the den doors were opened, the twins ran to tell their mother about it. Big Wool was with Friska and when she heard, she took Mary into a corner and looked at her mouth. Then she patted her very kindly on the shoulder and said if she'd just open her mouth wide, she'd pull the tooth out in a second, and the pain would stop, but

Mary backed away and shut her mouth tight, and wouldn't let Big Wool even look at it again.

Then Friska had an idea, and said excitedly, 'I know a lovely plan, it's like a game. We fasten a bit of thread to the tooth, and Mary sits down, and then we tie the other end to the door-handle, and we go out and slam the door after us hard, and out comes the tooth!'

Mary did not think *her* part sounded much like a game and said so, but Little Wool jumped up and down and said, 'Oh yes! Let's.'

'If Little Wool thinks it would be so much fun,' said Mary, 'why shouldn't he have it done first – he's biggest!'

'But Little Wool hasn't got toothache, and you don't pull out teeth unless they are bad,' explained Friska, and Little Wool breathed again.

After a great deal of discussion, Mary let them tie the thread on to the tooth and then attach it to the door.

'And now,' said Friska brightly, 'we'll all go out and bang the door, and when we come back the tooth will be gone.'

But it wasn't, for every time they pulled the door shut, Mary ran with it, and each time they rushed back to look, there she was, standing just inside, with the thread still on and the tooth still in. They tried it seven times and then gave up and untied the thread.

While they all sat round and wondered what to do next, Mary said suddenly, 'It's better!'

And everybody sighed with relief and hurried off to bed.

Chapter Six

Which begins with Mary and ends with Bunch

Something brown came shooting out of the den door into the Nursery, giving the twins, who were playing there, a great fright – because at first they did not see that it was Mary.

We must go back to early that morning. Mary as usual was the first up, and she wandered out into the nursery, sniffing and snuffing along the ground, and then she saw that the door leading into Big Wool's den was partly open.

Big Wool had not been seen for two whole days,

and the cubs had been told not to make too much noise as she had a headache.

Mary, seeing the door open, thought she would go and ask her how she was, so in she went. At first it was so dark that she thought it was empty. Big Wool was not there, and Mary was just turning to go when she spied two little round balls, covered with brown fur, lying on some straw. She was fond of exploring, so she advanced and poked one of them with her paw.

'Grrr –' said the ball. Mary backed away hastily. 'Grrr –' said the ball again, and Mary retreated still further and then stood, with head on one side and ears pricked.

'I beg your pardon,' she said politely.

'Grrr – grrr –' said both the balls together.

'Y-yes – of course,' said Mary – and fled.

Once safely in the nursery again, she could not get them out of her mind – such a strange noise for a ball to make – and she'd never seen a furry ball before. It was all very mysterious and she didn't like it much. But like it or not, after a few moments curiosity got the upper hand and she crept back to look again.

This time, just as she reached the odd things, Big Wool rose – immense and unseen in the gloom – and with a terrible roar she seized Mary by the scruff of her neck and pushed her out without a word of explanation.

The twins rushed up, full of enquiries and sympathy.

'Gracious, gracious!' they exclaimed. 'What has happened and why did you come out like that?'

'It wasn't on purpose,' said Mary.

She was still feeling upset when Friska came running in, a little later and said, 'Oh, cubs! Such a surprise. You've got two new little aunts! Isn't it lovely?'

So that was it!

'Would you like to come and have a peep? Big Wool says you may – and Mary too. Poor Mary's nose will be out of joint now.' Mary felt it hastily.

'Aren't you coming, Mary?' asked Friska.

'No, thank you,' said Mary, 'I like it here.'

Friska was surprised, but there was no accounting for Mary's moods, so she trotted off with a cub clinging to each paw.

Mary did some thinking when they were gone and when they came back she said, 'Then won't I be smallest any more?'

'No, of course not.'

'But if they are the twins' *aunts* how can they be smaller than me?'

'Because they are Big Wool's babies, don't you see?'

Mary didn't see. It was all very muddling, and altogether sickening. She had always been youngest and she didn't see why she shouldn't go on being it. So she decided to find a nice corner and have a sleep to see if that would make everything come right. She had great faith in sleep to solve problems – so much so, that when she woke later, she sat up and said, 'And am I still not the youngest?'

There was no one there to answer, for the twins were right at the other end of the pit. So Mary lay down again and yawned. She rolled over and there, within a few centimetres of her nose, lay a ball. Goodness, what a lot of them there were about today! But this was a paper one. Mary played with it idly, and then she noticed some writing on it, and soon she found she knew one of the words written there, which was Bunch. She scrambled up and trotted to the twins.

'Hey, look here, you two, I've found a ball with "Bunch" written on it.'

They all looked at it, and found it was made of lots of paper rolled together and all with writing on.

'Let's keep it and ask Mamma about it when she comes back,' said Marionetta. 'We're having a holiday today so she could read it to us.'

'Yes, let's!' said the others.

Now ever since Mary had got two names she insisted on being called both of them. The twins knew this and whenever they wanted to tease her, which was quite often, they would join hands and hop round her, singing:

'Ma-ry, Ma-ry,
Mary, Mary – P.
How we won-der
Whatyournamecanbe!'

and it never failed to make her angry.

They were full of impatience, on this morning, awaiting Friska's arrival, so that she could read them the story about Bunch, so, for lack of something better to do, they began this 'Mary' song.

Mary knew herself to be in a strong position, as she had the ball in question tucked under her right arm, so she said, 'Mary who, did you say, Little Wool?'

'Mary, Mary P,' sang Little Wool joyously.

Mary looked up at the wall and then took out the ball and looked at that. 'I daresay I could throw it over the wall – if I stood on the edge of the bath on tiptoe,' she said thoughtfully. The twins stopped dead, and Mary turned to Little Wool with a sweet smile, '*What* did I hear you say my name was, Little Wool?'

'Mary Plain,' said Little Wool earnestly, 'Mary Plain.'

'I hope you'll remember that,' said Mary.

'I'm quite sure I shall,' said Little Wool, with an anxious eye on the ball.

Mary went on looking first at the ball and then at the wall a few times – just to keep the twins in suspense, and then Friska came in and they all rushed up to her and begged her to read them what the ball said. So she unrolled it and read, and this is what it said:

THE POEM ABOUT BUNCH

I went down on Friday, just after my lunch.
'May I ask you some questions?' I asked
        my friend, Bunch.
His answer was vague – 'Pray, *have* you a carrot?
For I've not had a mouthful since dawn.'

I threw one, and said, 'Could you tell me, at length,
What you use for your coat, for its beauty and strength,
And' – 'Lick,' he said shortly, 'but *have* you that carrot?
For I've not had a mouthful since dawn.'

I said, 'Surely sitting cramped up on that tree,
Must give you lumbago and pains in your knee?'
'Appalling,' he groaned, 'but *have* you a carrot?
For I've not had a mouthful since dawn.'

'If you suffer so sadly, then why do you stay?
What is it that keeps you in torment all day?'
'Food!' he said frankly. 'Pray, *have* you a carrot?
For I've not had a mouthful since dawn.'

I remarked his companions looked hungry below,
'Now help me decide to which this one shall go.'
'Me!' said Bunch, promptly. 'Oh, *have* you a carrot?
For I've not had a mouthful since dawn.'

I dangled a carrot invitingly low,
And pretended I would, and then did not quite throw,
'I'm waiting,' sighed Bunch. 'Oh, *have* you a carrot?
For I've not had a mouthful since dawn.'

'I'll throw it,' I answered, 'if you'll whisper to me
If you'd rather 'twas biscuits, or cabbage, or tea.'
'Darn!' said Bunch rudely. 'Oh, *have* you a carrot?
For I've not had a mouthful since dawn.'

I explained his digestion quite soon would resist,
That the time might arrive when he'd *have* to desist.
'Never,' vowed Bunch, 'Oh, *have* you a carrot?
For I've not had a mouthful since dawn.'

'Mark my words,' I went on, 'it will soon go on strike!'
A remark, I'm afraid, that he did not quite like.
He replied, in tones icy, 'Pray, *have* you a carrot?
For I've not had a mouthful since dawn.'

I then did my best to impress him, with vigour,
That he'd better take care, or he'd soon lose his figure.
He stifled a yawn, 'Pray, *have* you a carrot?
For I've not had a mouthful since dawn.'

'Your greed, Mr Bunch!' I exclaimed with some heat,
'Would really require super-courage to beat.'
He brightened a little. 'Oh, *have* you a carrot?
For I've not had a mouthful since dawn.'

I threw him the last. 'Oh, Bunch, how you lie!
To speak but the truth I beseech you to try.'
He swallowed with haste – 'Pray, *have* you a carrot?
For I've not had a mouthful since dawn.'

As my steps bore me homeward, the sun shone
    in splendour,
And after me floated, by distance made tender,
The plaintive lament, 'Oh, *have* you a carrot?
For I've not had a mouthful since dawn.'

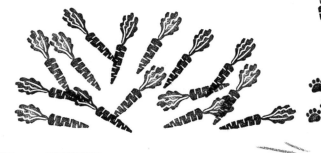

'Oh!' said the twins, 'fancy, Mary Plain, a poem about Bunch!'

'Oh!' said Mary Plain, 'fancy, Twins, a poem about Bunch!'

And, though Friska was much older, she too could find nothing better to say than, 'Dear, dear, dear, a poem about Bunch.'

'I wish it was about me,' murmured Mary. But nobody heard.

Chapter Seven

How Mary flew

Mary was having a difficult time getting to sleep again. She had collected all the words beginning with A she could think of, and she had counted backwards as far as she could go (which was down from five) several times, and then she had thought of all the things she would do the next day – but nothing seemed to help. In despair, she was just beginning to think of all the things she would *not* do the next day, when she heard a scratching noise at the door. The door was always left partly up at night so that the bears could get out into the pit if they wanted to, but there was a plank leaning across the open space to prevent the cold getting in.

At first Mary thought it was a burglar, and she was going to wake Friska, but then she decided it was too small a noise for a burglar to make, and she would be very brave and find out what it was, quite by herself. So she went to the door and leant down and said, just to be sure, 'Are you a burglar?' and a little voice said –

'No. I'm Robin.'

When she had pushed aside the plank, sure enough there was her friend Sir Robin.

'Hello,' he said. 'I had a kind of feeling you'd be awake, and I wondered if you'd care to come for a fly with me. It's a lovely night and not too cold.'

Mary was very surprised. 'But I can't fly,' she said.

'Oh, that will be quite all right. I'll sprinkle you with some shrinking powder I have and in two minutes you'll be the right size to ride me comfortably.'

'Will it hurt?' asked Mary anxiously.

'Of course not. If you'll look under the third feather in my left wing, you'll find a little blue packet, tied with a hair. That's right – thank you.' And he undid it and threw some yellow dust on Mary's head. She could never decide, afterwards, exactly what happened, but the next moment Robin looked so very big that Mary felt a little nervous of him.

'Now,' said he, briskly, 'just stand on the doorstep and you'll be able to reach, I think, and, if you feel a bit strange at first, just hang on to my neck feathers.'

Mary did as she was told, expecially the hanging on part, for, as they rose into the air, she did indeed feel very odd. After a few seconds she got used to it, and she began to look around and enjoy herself. It was really great fun to be sailing over the tops of the trees, almost as high as the moon, and what a lot of things there were to see in this wonderful outside world! For Mary had never been out of the pit, and she had only seen the same trees and the same bit of sky every day.

Presently Robin said, 'On the way back, I thought we'd stop in at my nest a moment; I'd like you to meet my wife, and then we've been invited to a meal at Berrrumperbotch Chalet. Of course you know Miss N, the lady who lives there? She wears a fancy coat.'

'N for what?' asked Mary.

'Ssh! N for Nothing,' said Sir Robin.

'Then must I call her Miss Nothing?' asked Mary.

'Psst!' said Sir Robin, and he looked anxiously at the tree they were passing, to see if anyone had overheard. 'Don't let me ever hear you say that again. Her name is Miss N and don't ask any questions.'

Mary sighed. She would have liked so much to know why. She thought privately that Berrrumperbotch was an odd name for a house, but she supposed Miss N must have some good reason for calling it that, and anyway, it would be delightful to see her.

They flew over a lovely green field, and here the sun was shining and the moon seemed to have disappeared.

Soon they came to a dear little pink house standing in a garden. Robin flew first to a big rose bush near the gate, where he lived with Lady Robin, but, as she was rather busy with three brand-new babies, they didn't stay long and moved on to the house.

'It's the colour of carrots,' said Mary, as they walked up the path.

'It *is* carrots,' said Sir Robin, 'and now, let me tell you one or two things, before we go in. First, be sure to walk in backwards; Miss N prefers it. And, let me warn you, that whenever she says "Wheazle!" whatever you are doing, you must get up, turn round three times,

and then bow. If you are not sure how to answer, just say, "Oh, what fun!" That always pleases her.'

Mary would have liked to ask a great many questions, but she had not even time for one, as, at that moment, they reached the door, and a voice called –

'Goodbye, goodbye, come in, don't.' And she turned round as she had been told and began to back in.

It was a little difficult getting over the doorstep, but Mary managed it all right. Then she stood up, and there was her friend of the fancy coat, and yet she was not quite the same. She was very small and had strange eyes and legs. Mary didn't like to stare; indeed she had no time, for the little lady hustled forward and opening a door, said, 'Just step into the bathroom, and I'll run and dish up the pebbles,' and she gave them a push into a room, which had a table in the centre, and a pile of umbrellas against the wall.

Mary looked round the room and underneath the table, but could see no sign of a bath, and before she could ask Sir Robin what it all meant, Miss N hurried back with a large dish, heaped with every kind of pebble – square ones, round ones, large ones, small ones, and all of different colours.

'Wet or dry?' she asked Mary.

'Dry, please,' said Mary, who didn't want any at all.

'Get me some milk, please, Robin,' she said next, 'not too warm.' And Mary watched Sir Robin go to the corner and turn on a tap, and, to her amazement, out came beautiful white milk, with which he filled a jug.

'Pull up that umbrella, bear, and make yourself comfortable,' and Mary fetched an umbrella and did her best to get settled on the handle. Miss N handed her some pebbles, but before Mary could say 'Thank you,' she snatched them away again, leant forward and said 'Wheazle!' very suddenly.

Mary almost fell off the umbrella, turned three times, made a bow, and sat down again, feeling very giddy, and said 'Oh, what fun!'

'He, he, he,' laughed the little lady, and then she dropped her voice, looked round the room, and said softly, 'Have some flies' wings on toast?'

'No, thank you,' said Mary, hastily.

Mary began not to like this place very much. 'He, he, he,' laughed Miss N, 'my father always had sandwiches of flies' wings when we went on picnics – very warming you know, and you need warmth, sitting on a cloud, for they're likely to be damp, very damp.' She looked at Mary fiercely. 'You understand that we never had another picnic after he was swallowed by the moon? No, we somehow lost heart after that – my poor mother felt it very much. What do you think, bear?'

Robin prodded Mary under the table, so she said, 'Oh, what fun!' which didn't seem quite the right answer. But it didn't matter, for Miss N clapped her hands and said 'He, he, he!' Then she got up, laid her finger on her mouth for silence, tiptoed to the door, looked out, closed it, and then went to the corner and beckoned mysteriously to Mary. Mary went, unwillingly, for she was feeling rather upset by this time. Miss N drew her close to her, till her mouth was touching Mary's ear, and then shouted 'Wheazle!' so loudly that Mary jumped. But she remembered her manners, turned round three times, and bowed. 'Well, well!' said Miss N impatiently and clapped her hands. 'Oh, what fun!' said Mary drearily.

At this Robin got up and said he thought they had better be going (and Mary felt sure he was right), so

Miss N said, 'Do have a cup of treacle before you go, just to cool you; it's so refreshing and it's boiling on the stove. Will you please get it, Sir Robin, because, you know – the fire – my legs – you understand.'

Mary glanced down and saw that Miss N's legs were made of sticks of barley sugar. Of course she did not dare go near the fire, for fear of their melting, poor thing. How awkward it must be, and how did she manage when there was no one there to help her? But she could never remember noticing about her legs before, and she had often seen them through the railings.

Robin came back, holding the cups, and, at that moment, Mary sneezed.

'Ah, now you've done it,' said Miss N. 'If anyone sneezes after the moon rises I'm bound to melt.'

'Melt!' said Mary. 'Do you mean your legs?'

'No, me – all of me.' And, as Mary stood there full of astonishment, she saw that Miss N's face was changing; her eyes, always odd, were now definitely figs, her nose was a carrot and her figure was white and round.

'You're the snowman we made the other day!' said Mary, but already the snowman was melting rapidly, and it only just had time to say, 'Ah, your ears, your ears!' before it all disappeared.

Mary's paws flew to her ears and sure enough, they had gone! 'Oh, oh, my ears, my ears!' she shouted. 'Oh! My ears, my ears!'

'Come, come, what's the matter?' said Friska's voice, and Mary found herself being shaken to and fro. She opened her eyes and there she was – back in her own den. How had she got there? She rubbed her eyes, but when she looked again, Friska was still there, so she must really be at home.

Then she felt for her ears. Yes, they were both there, so that was all right too. She sat looking very bewildered, wondering what it all meant.

Friska said, 'You'd better come along and have your breakfast, and that will wake you up, or perhaps you aren't hungry, and don't want any?'

'Oh, yes, I do!' said Mary, jumping up.

As she went through the door and saw the steam rising from her bowl, she smiled and said, happily, 'Oh, what fun!' and, for the first time, she meant it!

Chapter Eight

Full of planks, poles and Mary Plain

As soon as the morning cleaning routine was over, Mary hurried away. There were several things she wanted to find out. She had thought it all out during breakfast, and she really could not believe it had been only a dream. It was all so real, and she had been wide awake when Robin fetched her.

Of course, there was the question of her ears. They were back again, but then she could not remember anything about the journey back, so, for all she knew, they had grown again on the way, or, possibly,

Sir Robin had bought her a new pair. In any case, these were very comfortable, and that was all that mattered.

The first thing she set out to do was to see what came out of the tap which she'd noticed in Big Wool's den. If it was milk, then the tap at Miss N's was quite an ordinary one, but she somehow felt milk didn't usually come that way. While she was thinking about this she arrived at the den. The balls, or aunts, were now a little larger, but they still lay on the straw and did nothing but squeal, so Mary was not very interested in them any more, and just glanced at them as she went in.

She found she wasn't tall enough to reach the tap, so she pushed a barrel underneath and then climbed up on it and tried to turn the tap handle, but it was very stiff, and pull as she might, she couldn't move it. Then, just as she was giving up all hope, she gave an extra big pull, and it gave way, so suddenly, that Mary fell off the barrel, and out rushed a stream of water. Mary picked herself up and waited a few moments, to see if it would turn to milk, but it didn't, so she got up again to turn it off. Alas, this seemed to be just as hard as getting it to start, and after a short struggle, she gave it up, and said to herself, 'I don't expect there *can* be much more water in there, and then it will stop,' and she got down, went out and forgot all about it.

This was one of the mornings when the twins were playing games for two, so Mary amused herself by rolling over and over between the wall and the den door. She did it very fast, with her eyes shut, and the second time she reached the door, she felt it was rather damp, so she opened her eyes and got up, and there was a long stream of water running into the nursery.

This was serious, and Mary felt she must do something about it, so she ran along till she came to the door to Friska's den, where she and Big Wool were sitting, and said, 'I think you had better go and see in your den, Big Wool. I can't quite turn the tap off, and it's dripping a little.'

Big Wool sprang up, thinking of her babies and the colds they might catch, and hurried along to see. When she got there she found an absolute pond of water, with the tap full on, and she had a terrible fright. She pushed the handle back first and then rushed to her babies, and found them still on their bed of straw, which was floating about on the water. Luckily they were only a bit damp, and she moved them quickly into the next den and fussed over them till she got them dry.

Mary had been watching from the door, but when she saw Big Wool's face she thought it was time to disappear, so she went out to look for somewhere to hide. The nursery did not seem any good so she crept into her own den, got as far under the straw as she could and shut her eyes, hoping, if she found her asleep, Big Wool would not like to disturb her, because she had a feeling she would be looking for her very soon.

She was right. She heard Big Wool go out into the nursery and say in a furious growl, 'Mary Plain, come here immediately!' Then, when Mary did not come, she began looking for her. Mary heard her come in at the door, and kept her eyes very tight shut and hoped she didn't show. But the straw was rather transparent and Mary made rather a big lump, so she was found almost at once.

'How could you do such a naughty thing? How would you have felt if my babies had been drowned and it was all your fault?' shouted Big Wool.

'Glad,' thought Mary, but she didn't dare say so aloud.

'You are more naughty than I should have thought possible, and why didn't you come at once and tell me you couldn't turn the tap off?'

'I forgot,' said Mary sulkily.

'Oh! You forgot, did you? Forgot that those two helpless little cubs were lying there, in greater danger every moment! Well! You'll have plenty of time to think about it, because I shall lock both doors and you shall stay in here all day long, by yourself, and that may teach you not to forget, another time.' And with that Big Wool rushed out, locking the door behind her.

Those horrid cubs, what a nuisance they were! Mary thought to herself. This was the second time she'd got into trouble through them; and she had not done it on purpose. She wished to goodness Big Wool would not have babies. It seemed to make her lose her temper very easily.

Well here she was, so she would have to make the best of it. She got up and looked round to see what she could do. She began building a straw house, and that kept her very busy, till it all fell down on her and buried her, and that did not seem quite such fun. Then she found a piece of string tied on to a post, and trying to get it off took up another half-hour. But after that, there did not seem anything left to do, so she began to feel very bored, especially as she could hear Little Wool and Marionetta laughing outside in the nursery.

If only she could get out! She went and tried the doors, but they were firmly shut. Big Wool didn't do things by halves.

The only other place was a little window, high up in the wall, with the sun shining through it. What a dreadful pity it wasn't lower down, and she was taller, but it was so high up that even Big Wool could not have reached it, so Mary could only give a big sigh and turn her back, so as not to see the sun inviting her to go out. She walked over to the wall opposite, where three shelves were built, and for lack of something better to do, she started climbing up them. When she got to the top one, she saw a big beam over her head, so she swung herself up on to

70

this, and then found she was so high up she hardly dared to look down. Instead, she looked along it, and there, at the other end, right in front of her, was the little window. She could reach it after all! How exciting!

She crept very carefully along the beam till she got to the end, and there she found the window was unlatched, so all she had to do was to push it open and then she was looking down into the nursery which seemed a long way down below. She was just going to call out to the twins, who were playing with their backs towards her, when she saw a long plank tilted against the wall, just below the window sill. What wonderful luck, and she would give the twins such a surprise! So she climbed out, and sat on the top of the plank, and just before she let go of the sill, she called out, 'Here I am!'

As the twins swung round, they saw her come shooting down the plank, with ears flying.

'Mary, is it really you? But how did you get out? We were told you were locked in tight.'

'So I was, but I was tired of myself; so I climbed up to the window and got out, and oh! it's lovely sliding down the plank, and I must go and do it again. Come on, Little Wool, I'll show you how.'

They had a wonderful time, climbing up a drain pipe and coming down by the plank, one after the other. Indeed they made so much noise that, in Parlour Pit, Friska said to Big Wool, 'Do you hear those cubs of mine? They must be having a very exciting game.'

And Big Wool answered rather grimly, 'I hope Mary hears them too.' Little did she know that Mary was herself, at that moment, leading a glorious sliding party on the other side of the wall!

Mary could not help getting a little anxious toward evening, because she knew she would get into trouble for having escaped. Six o'clock came at last, and the doors were pulled up. Mary lingered in the nursery behind the others, but in a few moments, Marionetta came running back and said, 'Big Wool wants you at once in her den.' Mary heaved a heavy sigh.

Big Wool was standing just inside the door. 'Come here, Mary,' she said sternly. 'You were in disgrace this morning, but you are far, far more in disgrace tonight. Now go,' said Big Wool, and Mary went.

Next morning, however, straight after school, Mary was ready to do some more sliding.

She ran to the plank. 'Why, it's gone green in

the night. How funny!' she cried. 'Come on, Little Wool! I'll come down first and you next.' And she scrambled up the drain pipe and sat down on the plank. 'I'm off,' she said, and let go of the sill – but she wasn't. Instead of shooting down like a flash, there she was still at the top. 'I'm off!' she said again, and gave a little jerk – but no! She still wasn't. And, what was more, she couldn't if she wanted to; she was stuck – stuck tight onto the plank.

'Oh, twins, I'm stuck; I can't move!' she cried. 'Oh, come and pull me off; what can be the matter? It was so slippery yesterday and now the green has spoilt it all.'

Little Wool had, by this time, climbed up on a level with the window sill, and he leant over and pulled; but pull as he would, it was no good, and, struggle as she might, there she still was. As luck would have it, just at that moment along came Bunch's friend, the Owl Man.

He did not often come and see the cubs, and, naturally, they were very anxious to make a good impression, so Mary whispered, 'Stop pulling, and get down quick, till he's gone,' and then she crossed one leg over the other and tried to look as if it were quite usual to be sitting on a steep green plank.

'Hello, Mary Plain! What are you doing up there?' he called.

'Just sitting here for a bit.'

'Come down and do some jumping for me.'

'I'm too tired,' said Mary.

'Too tired at this time of the morning? Why?'

Mary yawned a very big yawn and said, 'Just because.'

'Well, well, well,' said the Owl Man, 'I think it's a very odd thing for a cub of your age to feel tired at this time of the morning – very strange. Are you sure you are feeling well?'

'Perfectly, thank you,' said Mary politely, and wished he would go.

But he didn't. He just stood and stared.

'Wouldn't you like to go and see Bunch?' suggested Mary.

'I've been,' said the Owl Man. 'Hey that plank's been painted; it wasn't green last time I was here, was it?'

'No,' said Mary, with a great deal of feeling.

'I thought not,' he said, 'the paint's a good colour – a nice shade of green.'

'Could you tell me,' asked Mary, 'is paint sticky?'

'Yes – especially when it's wet!' and then suddenly he understood. 'Oh no!' he said, 'you aren't stuck, are you?'

'I think I am!' said Mary.

'I *am* sorry,' said the Owl Man. 'Have you been there long?'

'Hours!' said Mary, who had been there exactly ten minutes.

'Then we must get you off as soon as we can. I wonder if I got a long stick, if I could reach you and pull you off.'

'Oh, please,' begged Mary. He went off, and in a few moments came back with a long pole, and leaning

over the wall, stretched as far as he
could and Mary just managed to
get hold of the other end.

'I am afraid it will hurt a bit,
but it's the only way,' said the
Owl Man, and pulled.

'Ow!' said Mary, but she was
away, and although her behind felt
uncomfortable, she was truly grateful
to the Owl Man, who was as nice as
could be, and gave her so much sugar that
Little Wool, who had been watching all the
time, wondered if it would be worth getting
stuck himself.

Later on that day, Mary, who had forgotten about
it, was dancing round and round for a carrot a little
girl was holding out for her. 'Oh, look!' cried the child,
'she's got a green back! Doesn't she look funny?'

Poor Mary tried to look, but could not manage
it, so she called Marionetta and said, 'Am I green
behind?'

'Yes, very,' said Marionetta, and then, thinking it
would please Mary, she repeated, '*Very* green indeed.'

Mary backed into a corner and sat down and there
she stayed the whole day – refusing all invitations to

jump or play. Nothing would move her till the doors were up at six, when she sidled along, with her back to the wall, into her den. Job heard about it when he brought the supper, and he very kindly washed all the green off with some special stuff. Although it burned and pricked, Mary was grateful, and promised him she would never again slide down a plank.

'At least not a green one,' she added to herself.

Chapter Nine

In which Mary behaves her best

Job walked into the dens one afternoon and pulled open one of the doors leading into the nursery.

'Come here, Mary Plain,' he called, 'I have to tell you something.'

Mary came running and so did the twins, because Job never visited them during the day, and they couldn't imagine what he wanted.

When Mary was sent for, it usually meant she'd got into trouble, so she said half anxiously, 'I haven't been sliding down the plank, and I'm not a bit green. See?' And she turned round.

Job laughed. 'You're a funny one,' he said. 'But I want you here to give your coat a good brush, because you've been invited out to tea.'

Mary's eyes grew round.

'Me – out to tea? Who with? Where? Oh – why?'

'Why not us?' said the twins.

'I can't say, I'm sure. Perhaps two cubs together would be too many; and as to who, it's a kind lady who is interested in you all, but she sent the invitation specially to Mary. Come along now, we must hurry up and leave or we shall be late.'

Mary stuck her chest out as far as it would go. She was the youngest, and had been invited out to tea, and nothing as exciting had ever happened to any of them before. It even made her feel a little sick.

'Goodbye, Twins,' she said grandly, and waved her paw. 'I hope you won't miss me too badly but I daresay I'll be back some day. I'm sorry you weren't invited. But I'm glad it was me,' she added to herself.

Job brushed her till her coat was lovely and smooth and she tingled all over, and then he put on a collar and lead round her neck, which Mary didn't much like, but he explained that bears always had to wear them when they went out to tea, and especially in trams.

They climbed up some stairs and came out of a door at the top, and Mary, looking through the railings, could see the twins in the nursery down below, looking very dull and sad. She called down, 'My coat is all shiny and now I am going in a tram – so goodbye!' This was just to cheer them up a little. The twins didn't know what a tram was, but they longed to go in one.

When the first tram came rattling up and Mary was told to get in, she felt a little nervous, but Job got in first and seemed quite used to it, so she plucked up courage and followed him. A man came along and Job said, 'One and a half, please.'

'Bears fourpence,' said the man.

'But she's under seven months,' said Job.

'Bears twopence extra,' said the man firmly, so Job sighed and Mary sat down feeling very important about being extra. While they were going along, Job explained to her that she must be careful to remember her manners – shake hands with her right paw, say, 'thank you' and 'please'.

'Back or front paw?' asked Mary.

'Front, of course; and you must stand up nicely when you are introduced to people.'

'What's "introduced"?'

'It's saying "How d'you do" to someone you don't know, and being told their name.'

'I see,' said Mary, who didn't in the least. 'Do I have to walk in backwards?' she went on, while vague memories of Berrrumperbotch Chalet stirred, 'and do we have pebbles to eat?'

'Gracious me!' said Job, 'what is the cub thinking of? You'll probably have cake and biscuits, and milk to drink; but remember you must never eat anything until you are asked.'

'Asked how?'

'Well, till someone says, "Would you like some cake or biscuits." And then you say, "Yes, please" and take some.'

'Of course,' said Mary.

They changed trams once, just opposite the big fountain with the bears carved on it. Mary caught sight of them, and started jumping up and down and pulling Job towards them.

'Oh, Mr Job, there are the twins. I must go and speak to them.' Job pulled her back sharply and looked quite startled. But then he saw what she was looking at and said, 'It's not the twins, and don't go pulling and jumping like that and making a scene.'

'What's "a scene"?'

'What you're doing – making people look at you.'

'But don't they like looking at me?' Just then the other tram came up, so Job didn't have to answer.

Nearly all the streets in Berne are arcaded, with shops under the arcades, so you can do your shopping on rainy days and walk nearly all over the town without getting wet. A great many people have flats over them and the family Mary was going to visit lived in a large one on the second floor.

When they got out of the tram they turned a corner, and went through a big door and got into a lift.

When Job pressed the button they began to go up, and Mary thought it was most thrilling.

'Have I flown?' she asked, as she stepped out. But Job only laughed and pressed a button in the wall, and this time it didn't make them move, but it made a funny tingling noise through the wall.

The door was opened and a man with shiny buttons on his coat said, 'Will you come in, please?' Job pushed Mary in, in front of him and took off her collar, and then he whispered, 'Don't forget – the right paw!'

They had to walk down a passage so Mary said, 'Right, left, right, left,' to herself all the way, so as to be sure not to forget. Only somehow she must have got muddled on the way, because when she got into a room at the end, which seemed to be full of people, she held up the paw which she thought was the right. Job pulled it down and hissed – 'Wrong paw, Mary. Mind your manners.'

A tall lady in grey came up and said, 'How do you do?' and shook her paw.

'How do you do?' said Mary. 'I came by tram, twopence extra.'

'Oh, she is charming,' cried the lady to several others who were standing by her.

'No, not charming!' said Mary. 'Plain – Mary

Plain.' Then she was suddenly surrounded by lots of ladies, who wanted to pat her and stroke her, and seemed really delighted that she had come. Mary began to feel a great success.

'Well, now – how about tea?' asked the Grey Lady. 'Are we all ready?'

'I am!' said Mary.

'Jill hasn't come,' said another lady.

'Never mind, we'll begin without her. There's the bell. I expect that's her.'

It wasn't her, but it *was* the Owl Man, and Mary beamed. He shook hands with her and then bent down and said, 'How's the paint?' But Mary looked round anxiously to see if anyone had heard and then said, 'Hush, that's a secret.'

'Of course,' said the Owl Man.

'If you're all ready, come along to the dining room,' said the Grey Lady, and then turning to Job, 'Will she be all right if you leave her with us?'

'I'm sure she will, madam; and if you need me you can give me a call,' and he went off to find Thomas, who had opened the door to them, but, as he passed Mary, he said in a low voice, 'Now, Mary, manners!'

Mary was led to the table and shown to a chair next to the Grey Lady.

'Come and sit down and we'll begin,' she said. 'I expect you are getting hungry?'

'I am,' said Mary frankly.

'Well, you must eat all you can. Let me help you onto your chair.' But Mary drew back suddenly.

'No, thank you – I like to stand,' she stammered, with her eyes fixed on the chair which was a very bright green leather.

'But you can't possibly reach.'

'Oh, yes, but I don't want to, thank you.'

'Let me help you to jump up. You'll be far more comfortable.'

'No, please – I mean thank you, oh dear, oh dear,' said Mary getting more and more worried and then, all at once, she remembered the Owl Man was there, quite close to her; so she pulled him into the corner and when he bent down, whispered, 'Is it paint – please?'

He might have laughed, but he didn't. He just patted her on the head and said, 'No, I promise you. Here, I'll give you a lift up,' and with that, he swung her up and landed her with a bump on the chair, and she wriggled with happiness.

There on her plate was a lovely piece of cake and, beside the plate, a big bowl of creamy milk.

Mary had to sit on her paws because she was so afraid she'd begin before she was asked.

The Grey Lady said, 'I hope you like cakes?'

'Yes, yes,' said Mary, 'oh *very* much.'

'That's good! Then I hope you'll enjoy it.'

'I am *sure* I shall,' said Mary.

'It's a home-made cake and very delicious,' went on the Grey Lady, wondering why she didn't begin.

'It looks *too* lovely,' said Mary, with a little gasp.

'There is some sugar icing on that piece – perhaps you don't like it?' said the Grey Lady, getting very puzzled.

'Oh – I do – I do!' sighed Mary, and sat tight on her paws that were trying to get out. If *only* someone would say the words that Job had told her to wait for, so she could begin.

Just then a girl with a red frock leant forward and said, 'Would you like some cake?' and Mary adored

her for it, and said, 'Oh, thank you, I will!' At last she could eat it.

She had a great many cakes, and she was just finishing off a beautiful pink sugar carrot, when the door opened, and in walked the Fancy-Coat-Lady and everybody said 'Hello, Jill.' Mary was delighted and scrambled down and went to meet her. 'How do you do?' she said. 'I came by tram, twopence extra.'

'Did you indeed?' said the lady. 'Well that must have been fun!'

'It was,' said Mary and sighed happily.

By this time she was very full of cake and sweets and she had drunk all the milk she wanted, which was a great deal, so perhaps it was a good thing when the Grey Lady said, 'Let's go back into the other room, because I promised that my little girl would meet Mary after tea.'

Back they all went and presently the door opened and a little tiny girl came in. Mary didn't know how small little girls could be and she hoped she wouldn't be at all like the aunts. But she turned out to be very nice and they made friends at once.

Then Jill asked if they would like to play 'Hide-and-Seek'. The Owl Man hid Mary in a beautiful place under the sofa, but the minute he left her, she started shouting, 'I'm here, I'm here!' till they found her, which was almost at once, so they changed the game to 'I spy'. But Mary wasn't very good at this game because she was busy looking for the 'Ice pie'.

After that, the Grey Lady rang a bell and Thomas came to the door, and she said, 'Will you bring some milk and biscuits please?' He did and Mary thought Thomas was a delightful man. Then Job came in and said it was time to go home and he whispered, 'Be sure to shake hands nicely and thank her for having you.'

'No – no – just bow,' whispered Mary, who was standing with her arms very straight down.

'I said "Shake hands",' said Job sternly and gave her a little push forward. So Mary went up to the Grey Lady and said, 'Thank you for having me.' When she held her hand out, Mary knew she would have to shake it, so she lifted her paw – and out tumbled five biscuits which she had tucked under her arm!

The Grey Lady was very surprised, because she thought Mary had been given enough tea. However, as she was so nice, she didn't say anything, but stooped to pick them up. But, when Mary moved to help and six more tumbled out from under the other arm, Mary began to think perhaps it wasn't quite normal to take other people's biscuits away from a party and she'd better explain, so she whispered, 'They were for the twins.'

90

And the lady smiled and said, 'Of course – I ought to have thought about that,' and she told Thomas to get a big paper bag and fill it with biscuits.

Mary smiled happily and shook hands again, and said, 'Thank you for having me,' and then waited, as if she expected something.

Job came forward, after a moment and said, 'Come along, Mary, are you dreaming? We must be off home.' And they went – Mary clasping the paper bag tightly.

'Why did you wait like that after you said goodbye?' asked Job curiously.

'I was waiting for the lady to thank me for coming.'

'It was very kind of her to ask you.'

'Wasn't it kind of me to go, then?' asked Mary. But Job didn't seem to know.

Chapter Ten

St Bruin's day – and the last

The great day had come at last. After breakfast Big Wool stood up and cleared her throat and said, in a very serious way –

'Bears! This is St Bruin's Day, and I hope we all realize, *all* realize – Mary,' she said, because Mary didn't seem to be listening very attentively, 'how great an occasion this is. We shall take very special care with our cleaning and tidying this morning, and at six we shall meet again to have a final brush up.' (Mary sighed loudly.) 'In the meantime, I ask you all to pass the day in a fitting manner.' She was so pleased with the last sentence, that she gave a little cough, and repeated, 'in a fitting manner'.

'I think that is all I have to say – except that, when we all meet this evening before waiting on our – on our – ancestors,' said Big Wool, getting a little muddled, 'you will, of course, all bring with you the small presents you have put aside.'

This brought Mary to full attention. Gracious Heavens! She hadn't got a present. Last night she'd had one – a beautiful juicy carrot with the leaves still on – how juicy it had been she was, alas, in a position to know only too well – because, to stop a strange 'asking' feeling in her waist, she had eaten that carrot in the small hours of the morning.

Only now did she realize what a terrible thing she had done. There wasn't the slightest hope of getting another such carrot. It was the biggest she'd ever seen and it was pure luck that it had fallen to her, so beautifully – just the day before St Bruin's Day, and she had been so proud and pleased and guarded it in a corner all day. Oh dear, oh dear, she must have been mad, and indeed she had been half asleep.

She collected frantically all morning, and at midday retired to a corner and examined her store.

One faded carrot stalk, two very small figs, half a biscuit, and an empty glass bottle; oh – and a cork. She sat down and eyed them sadly. She was quite certain the carrot stalk and the figs wouldn't do and she felt sure that neither Alpha nor Lady Grizzle would appreciate half a biscuit, especially as she knew for a fact that Marionetta had a whole one she'd saved from last week. No! It was between the bottle and the cork. Suddenly she pounced on the bottle – a hole in it! If only the cork would fit! Her paws shook with excitement as she tried to persuade the cork into a hole half as big as itself – but she soon threw them both away in disgust.

Then she thought of developing a sudden cold, so she went and stood just under the wall which divided the nursery from Parlour Pit, and sneezed for ten minutes. But, alas, they can't have been very good imitations because she distinctly heard Big Wool say to Friska, 'Listen to those cubs. They must be playing at doctors, for one of them is pretending to have a cold.' So that was no good.

Then she thought of breaking her leg, and her eyes got quite misty with tears of self-pity, as she pictured herself being carried into the presence of the two ancients by Friska and Bunch and hearing them explain, 'This poor little cub has broken her leg, but she is so extremely brave about it, in fact we have never seen anyone quite so brave before.' They would be so sorry for her and so proud of her courage, that they would forget to expect a present from her.

Yes – the leg idea seemed far the best, but just as she was wondering what was the best way to set about it, a strange kind of whistle made her look up at the railings above. At that very moment she saw a little boy there open his mouth to speak, and out dropped something which fell into the pit, close to Mary. He seemed upset at having lost it and wanted to climb over to fetch it, but his mother didn't seem to want him to do this. Mary thought to herself, 'If he's so unhappy at losing it, it must be something rather important – perhaps a tooth,' and she picked it up and had a look. It wasn't a tooth at all. It was round and small and shiny, like silver, and had a hole in the middle, but, though she licked it, it didn't have any taste. However she'd decided it must be a kind of sweet, for the boy had it in his mouth. At any rate, that settled it. She'd take it to the two old bears, and if they didn't like it she couldn't help it – it was the best she could do, and at least it was shiny. So she went and hid it under a loose stone in the corner of the pit, to keep it safe till the evening.

'What *are* you going to do about your present?' asked the twins, later on, because Mary had told them about the carrot. 'Won't you be frightened to go without anything?'

'But I've got something,' said Mary casually.

'Oh, what?'

'Something, I said.'

'Oh, but do tell us what.'

'No, it's a secret,' and she kept it all day.

As soon as the doors were up, all the business of getting tidy had to be gone through again, and Mary was sick of it, and very thankful St Bruin's Day only came once a year. At the end they all stood up and recited the poem they had been learning in school all that week, to be sure they had it quite right. It went like this:

> *Many happy years we wish to you,*
> *May carrots and dried figs your pit-floor strew,*
> *We hope that happiness will with you stay*
> *Till we all meet on next St Bruin's Day.*

By Friska'

'Be sure not to forget to say "by Friska", will you?' said Friska anxiously — she was so very proud of having written the poem — and they all promised to remember.

Then Mary slipped away and rushed to the corner where she had hidden her present. She felt quite anxious as she lifted the stone, in case anyone had stolen it, but it was still there safe and sound and she breathed a sigh of relief and popped it into her mouth. That was where the small boy had kept it, so obviously it was the safest plan to do the same. She was so quick that no one had noticed her absence, and she got back just in time to hear Big Wool say, 'Now, are we all ready? And don't forget to bow!' And it began to be quite exciting.

Mary felt her heart going pit-a-pat and she stood up very straight and tried to turn her feet out. Unfortunately Little Wool spoke to her just as she was stepping over the doorstep into Den Pit, and she caught her paw and fell in flat on her face. However, Friska, who was in front, picked her up quickly and smoothed her down, so no real damage was done.

It is true she had *very* nearly swallowed her present, but, as she had not *quite* done so, it did not matter.

Now the cubs had heard these two old bears talked

about a great deal and they had been told they were very wonderful and wise and knew everything there was to know, and as they had heard all this and yet had never seen them they seemed all the more mysterious. When Mary's turn came she determined to make a very good impression.

Alpha was sitting on the edge of the bath to receive them and Lady Grizzle stood just beside him.

'You now,' said Friska, who was standing at the side and telling them each when their turn came.

Mary stepped forward and made a really beautiful bow. Then she took a deep breath, opened her mouth and out came, not the expected poem, but a piercing whistle. Mary looked very surprised and so did all the others, and they looked round to see if anyone

else had come into the pit. But no one had, so Mary tried again and the same thing happened, so then she knew it must be herself. This time, however, she was determined to get through the poem, so she went on, whistling bravely till Friska, who saw Alpha was getting angry, came and pulled her away. She whispered to Bunch to go and say the poem again, and to go on saying it till she told him to stop, so as to keep Alpha busy. Then she led Mary into the farthest corner and said, 'Don't you feel very well, Mary?'

'Wheee –' whistled Mary.

Friska was alarmed. This was serious. She had heard of people losing their voices during a bad cold, but never of their making a noise like this, and besides, Mary had not had a cold. She put her arm round her and said kindly, 'Tell Auntie where it hurts, Mary dear?'

'Wheee –' went Mary.

Every time she made this extraordinary sound, Friska looked anxiously to see if Alpha had heard, but Bunch was saying the poem in such a loud voice, that she did not think he could have.

'There, there, there,' she said, soothingly. 'I'm sure it will soon be better,' and she rubbed Mary's tummy gently. But Mary shook her head violently and pushed her paw away. 'Wheee –. Wheee –. Wheee –!' she whistled earnestly.

Friska said, 'Shh' again, and then looked at her helplessly. It was so like Mary to go and get unwell on this most important day, and such an odd kind of illness, too. She might at least have chosen a silent one, or one that could be understood and cured like a sore throat or a tummy-ache.

Just then Big Wool hurried up and Friska drew her on one side and explained. 'I know,' said Big Wool, capably, 'a firm hand. Leave her to me!' and she nodded her head knowingly. Then she came to Mary, clapped her paws sharply, and said, 'Come, come, Mary, enough of this nonsense! Just stop making that noise and behave yourself. I can't imagine what you –'

'Wheee –' interrupted Mary. Big Wool stood and blinked and then she turned Mary slowly round, while she felt her carefully all over. But she could not find anything wrong.

Now Mary was getting rather tired of all this fussing, so she decided she would go and give Alpha his present and give up trying to say the poem again, and she started off towards him. Directly Big Wool and Friska saw where she was going they rushed after her and, each taking a paw, they led her firmly back into the corner. 'Wheee –!' said Mary, trying to explain, but Friska put her paw over her mouth and said, 'Shh! Shh! Quiet, Mary, quiet.' And Big Wool stroked her in long soothing strokes down her back, which Mary hated, but she could not speak, so she had to bear it.

'Shall we take her home?' suggested Big Wool, but at this Mary whistled so loud and so long that it took them some moments to silence her. When she was quiet again, Friska beckoned to Big Wool and said in a low voice, 'Perhaps she'll take a sudden turn for the better?' But Big Wool shook her head. 'I doubt it, I doubt it,' she said, 'it looks very bad to me.'

While they were talking, Mary took the opportunity to escape again, and this time she got to within a few feet of Alpha before Friska caught her and dragged her back again.

'Oh dear, oh dear, what *can* we do?' she said to Big Wool. 'We can't go on like this. What do you suggest?'

Mary turned away and putting her paws behind her back, she kicked the ground a bit, to show she did not know they were talking about her.

'How about a slice of cake?' said Big Wool, and

Friska trotted off briskly to fetch one. When she brought it back, Mary suddenly felt so hungry that she forgot all about the little thing in her mouth and took a huge bite of cake. Then she choked and choked and they had to pat her on the back and finally shake her by the heels and, as they did this, out dropped something which fell with a tinkle on the ground and rolled away.

'Let me go, let me go,' shrieked Mary, kicking for all she was worth, and Big Wool was so surprised at hearing her speak again that she let go rather too quickly and Mary fell with a thud on to the floor. But she scrambled up, rushed to pick up the little disc, and before anyone could stop her, she had flown across the pit to Alpha's seat. Now Bunch was just saying the poem for the thirty-second time, in a rather hoarse voice, and Alpha was so sick of it that he was almost glad of any interruption – even Mary.

She was a little out of breath when she reached him. 'Here is your present, and oh please take it because it's so little and I am afraid of losing it and I do hope you'll like it,' she said, all in a rush – and laid it on his knee.

Alpha looked at it. 'Is this a practical joke?' he asked sternly.

'Oh, no,' said Mary, 'it's a kind of noise and you keep it in your mouth.'

Alpha did not look as if he believed it, but he placed it in his mouth all the same, and sure enough out came a low whistle. He took it out hastily. 'Is that me, or is it still you making that noise?' he asked Mary suspiciously.

'No, sir, it was you,' said Mary.

Alpha looked again at the round thing in his paw; and putting in into his mouth he blew, and out came another splendid whistle. A slow, broad smile crept over his face, and he sat down and blew and whistled and whistled and blew for several minutes, looking more and more pleased.

Then he beckoned Mary to him and patting her on the shoulder said, 'Well, well, my cub, you have brought me a most interesting present, and I am very pleased, very pleased.'

So Mary's gift was the greatest success after all, and, when they went away that evening, they left Alpha sitting happily under the tree, blowing the whistle as loud as he could.

It had been altogether a rather tiring day, and when they got home the bears found they were all very ready for bed. Just as the cubs had got tucked up all together, Little Wool said,

'Wasn't it awful when Mary wasn't well?'

'Mary who?' asked Mary, sleepily.

'Mary Plain,' said Little Wool.